# Not My Hat

written by Jennifer Jacobsen

illustrations by Jeff Lees

Stay Safe!
~
Jennifer
Jacobsen

I dedicate this book to my husband and two sons. Thank you for your encouragement and support.

I want to thank my parents for teaching me about the dangers of strangers.

Kristen was a happy little girl. She enjoyed riding her bike, reading books, writing stories, swimming, playing with toys, and going to school. Traveling was something else Kristen enjoyed doing. Going to the beach was her favorite place to go with her family.

One time, Kristen, her mom, her dad, and her little sister went on vacation to Florida. They had a wonderful time playing at the beach, visiting new places and even picking oranges from trees in an orange orchard.

Like many trips the family took, Kristen came home with a prized souvenir: a tan, straw cowboy hat with colorful pom-poms dangling from the rim. Embroidered on the front on the hat was the word "FLORIDA." Kristen LOVED that hat! She wore it everywhere. She would have slept with it on if she could have.  She told her parents, "I love my Florida hat so much, and I am not going to ever get rid of it."

Other places she traveled to were historical places where she learned lots of new things about different time periods in history. She liked learning, so when her parents taught her how to be safe, she listened.

For example, her mom would say, "Don't touch the stove when it is on. You will burn yourself."

Kristen's dad would warn her, "Look both ways before you cross the street."

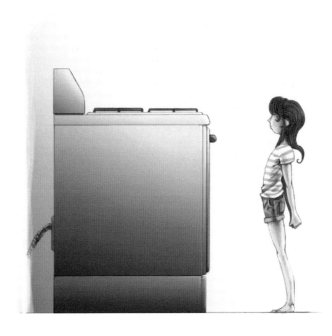

Kristen learned many valuable and life-saving lessons from her parents. Even as a young child, Kristen knew which ways were north, south, east, and west. She knew her left from her right, and she could understand what a map was used for.

Another lesson Kristen's parents had taught her was *never, ever* talk to strangers. *Never* take candy or toys from someone she did not know. *Never, ever* get in a stranger's car, truck, van, SUV, or go into a stranger's house. *Never, ever* open the front door of her home to someone she did not know. *Never, ever* talk to strangers.

**NO MATTER WHAT.**

Kristen knew a stranger was a man or woman she did not know. She knew a stranger could be nice and friendly. Kristen learned that she could not identify a stranger by their looks alone.

One cloudy afternoon, Kristen took a stroll down her suburban street, walking only as far as her parents permitted her to go on her own.  And of course, she had on her much-loved Florida hat.

A few houses down from her house, an old man with white hair and an unshaven face pulled up beside her on the street in a light blue pickup truck. Dents and rust were all over the truck, and the back was full of junk.

Kristen stopped walking when the man politely asked her if she knew the way to the airport. Kristen shook her head no, even though she knew the airport was in the opposite direction he was headed. She wondered why he would be looking for an airport in a neighborhood.

With a gruff voice the man said, "I like your hat. Did you get that in Florida?" Her hat? He liked her hat? Kristen knew not to speak to him so she stood, frozen, thinking hard about what her next move should be. "Come on over to my truck so I can see the hat better. I really like it and would like to buy it from you. Come on over to my truck so I can get a closer look at your hat."

Kristen panicked and was angry that someone would ask to buy her hat. How dare he!

Kristen knew not to talk to strangers, and she also knew to make loud

noises or commotion to try to get someone's attention. She yelled, "NO!

MY HAT IS NOT FOR SALE!" Kristen immediately ran home in the

opposite direction from the man and his beat-up old pickup truck. She

did not even turn around to see if the man was following her. She ran

and ran as fast as she could.

She burst in the front door of her home, and, without taking a breath, Kristen repeated the story to her mom. Her mom called the police because she knew Kristen had just been approached by a stranger, and the police needed to be looking for the old man. Kristen was scared. Had she done something wrong? She thought she was supposed to run home or to another safe place, and tell a trusted adult about a stranger. Was the police officer going to take her to jail? She was really frightened.

Soon, a police officer knocked on Kristen's front door. Kristen's mom let him in. He looked friendly. He smiled and greeted both Kristen and her mom warmly. At first, the officer and Kristen's mom talked. Then the officer took off his hat and faced Kristen, and said, "I like your hat. Did you get that in Florida?"

Even though she did not know this man, he was a police officer, and he was a safe person to talk to. But she could not help wondering if now this man wanted her hat too.

"Yes. I got it in Florida. But it's not for sale!" Kristen announced.

"I don't want to buy your hat, Kristen. I know it is special to you. I just want you to tell me everything you remember about the man who wanted to buy your hat."

Kristen had a great memory and could remember everything from the scary time earlier that day.

She explained she had been walking down the street and how an old, unshaven man in a light blue, rusty pickup truck had asked her where the airport was. "I don't understand why he was asking where the airport was. He was driving the wrong way. The airport is that way," she said as she pointed the correct direction toward the airport. The police officer wrote in a little note pad as Kristen talked.

When she was done retelling the story, Kristen was proud for being honest and remembering so much important information. But she was still worried.

"Am I going to jail now? Did I do something wrong?" Kristen asked the officer, frightened he would say, "Yes."

The officer got down on one knee, looked straight into Kristen's scared, blue eyes and said, "Absolutely not. You did a wonderful thing today. Your love of your hat probably saved your life. If you had not been so fond of your hat, you may have been more willing to go to that man's truck, and he might have taken you," the officer explained. "No, Kristen, you did the right thing. You knew not to approach a stranger no matter what he was offering you. I'm proud of you. You did the right thing. The safe thing. And I'm sure your parents are proud of you too. You are not going to jail." The policeman smiled, and Kristen breathed a sigh of relief.

Kristen understood that she had made a safe choice that day, a choice that may have saved her life.

The police officer and Kristen's mom continued to talk as Kristen dashed off to play—wearing her dearly loved Florida hat.

# Stranger Danger Discussion Prompts and Tips

- From an early age, explain that a stranger is someone we do not know. Some strangers are very nice. Strangers dress and look like we do.

- Many strangers who want to hurt children try to lure children to them by offering them candy or a toy. Stress to your child that even though they may really desire the bait, never to take it.

- Make sure your child feels safe to come to you or another trusted adult in case of a stranger situation. Try to get them to share as many details as possible.

- Always get the authorities involved if your child comes to you with a stranger situation. Praise the child for being honest and coming to you. Encourage them to tell the police everything they remember.

- Inform your child that firefighters and police officers are safe strangers.

- Have a secret family password that only your family knows. Use it when someone other than you is picking your child up from school, a sporting event, scouts, etc. Have the child ask the adult the password. If the adult does not know the password, instruct your child not to go with them.

- Find safe neighbors they can run to in case they need a safe get away.

- Instruct children to always run in the opposite direction a stranger and run to someone safe.
- If a stranger is confronting the child, have the child scream as loud as they can, "You are not my mom!" or "You are not my dad!" or "FIRE!" Have them keep screaming until a safe adult comes to their rescue, or the stranger goes away.
- Get a silicone wrist band that you can write your cell number and any other safe contact's phone number on so if separated, a safe adult your child has gone to knows how to contact you.
- Go to your local police station and get a DNA pack. Keep this pack in a fire proof safe or safe deposit box. Prepare two or three kits and give one to a grandparent, aunt, uncle, trusted family friend, etc. in case you cannot get to your kit in an abduction situation.

You can never completely prepare for a child abduction, but you can take precautions. These discussions and organizational tips are uncomfortable sometimes, but remember they could save your child's life one day.

# Epilogue

This is a true story about me. I grew up hearing about stranger danger and what to do if a stranger came near me. In this case, I believe my life was saved because I followed what my parents taught me about strangers.  I hope and pray every child who reads this story will learn about stranger danger.  To this day, I do not know if the old man was ever caught by the police even though, I gave such a detailed report about my encounter with him. I do believe that calling the police was the right thing to do.

Made in the USA
Charleston, SC
27 March 2015